Noddy and
the Artists

Collins

An Imprint of HarperCollinsPublishers

NODDY

CLOCKWORK MOUSE

BIG-EARS

MARTH

TESSIE BEAR

GOBBO

MR PLOD

MASTER TUBBY BEAR

ONKEY

SLY

MR WOBBLY MAN

BUMPY DOG

It was a sunny day in Toyland . . .

Noddy had nearly run out of petrol, so he had driven his little car to Mr Sparks' garage.

"I won't be a minute, Noddy," Mr Sparks told him. "I'm just finishing this painting of Miss Pink Cat."

"I never knew you were a great artist, Mr Sparks!"
Noddy said with admiration as he walked round to look
at the painting.

"Oh, Mr Sparks is a brilliant artist!" exclaimed
Miss Pink Cat. "All the toys will wish to see his paintings,
so we shall have a show tomorrow in Market Square!"

The exhibition was a huge success. "It looks just like Miss Pink Cat!" Jumbo exclaimed and all the other toys agreed.

Indeed, everyone was so impressed by Mr Sparks' pictures that they wanted to try their hand at painting as well!

Noddy went straight to Dinah Doll's stall. "Do you sell paints and brushes, Dinah?" he asked her eagerly.

"For painting your house?" she asked. "Yes, I have plenty of paints and brushes, Noddy."

"No, I want them for painting pictures," Noddy explained.

Mr Tubby Bear also came to Dinah Doll's stall. So did Clockwork Mouse and many of the other toys. Everyone wanted artists' paints and brushes!

"I'm sorry!" Dinah Doll said, rather flustered. "I just don't sell that type of paint or those brushes!"

"Psst! Noddy!" Sammy Sailor whispered, secretly taking him aside. "Years ago I picked up a cargo of artists' paints and brushes on one of my voyages. If you help me sell them, I'll share the money we make!"

"What a good idea, Sammy Sailor!" Noddy exclaimed. "Everyone in Toy Town wants paints and brushes at the moment so we should sell lots and lots of them!"

Noddy and Sammy decided to set up a new stall in Market Square to sell their paints and brushes.

Noddy walked round with a special board to let all the toys know about the stall.

"Good day, Noddy!" Clockwork Mouse greeted him. "What has happened to your legs?"

"They're under this board!" Noddy chuckled. "Will you tell everyone to come to Sammy's stall, Clockwork Mouse?"

Soon there was a long queue at Sammy Sailor's stall.

"I can't wait to get started on my painting," Mr Tubby Bear said excitedly, as he walked away from the stall with an armful of paints and brushes.

"Nor can I!" said Clockwork Mouse, who was next in the queue.

"What wonderful business I'm doing!" Sammy Sailor thought to himself. "At this rate, I'll soon have no more paints or brushes left!"

Dinah Doll was far less happy, though. Her stall had
not had a single customer all day!

"Since Sammy Sailor opened his stall," she told Tessie
Bear miserably, "toys no longer seem to want the
ordinary things that I sell!"

That evening, while Noddy was painting a picture of Tessie Bear, she told him about Dinah Doll's sad plight.

"I'm very worried about Dinah Doll," she explained. "All the toys are so busy painting they've stopped going to her stall. If nobody buys anything she won't be able to keep it running!"

"Why, that's awful!" Noddy exclaimed. "And it's partly my fault because I helped Sammy Sailor set up his stall!"

"First thing tomorrow," he added firmly, "I'll go to Dinah Doll's stall and buy something there, even if I don't want it!"

However, when Noddy went to Dinah Doll's stall in the morning, he found that it was closed!

"It looks as if it's closed for good!" Noddy said to himself in alarm. "Poor Dinah must have decided to leave Toy Town!"

"Where's Dinah Doll?" Miss Pink Cat asked. "I want to buy something pretty from her to decorate my house. It's no good going to Sammy Sailor's stall. He's now trying to sell all the toys' paintings – but every single one of them is quite horrid!"

Noddy marched right up to Sammy Sailor's stall.

"You'll never sell those horrid paintings, Sammy!"
Noddy told him firmly. "We just want Dinah Doll back
so we can buy nice things again. Don't we, everyone?"

Everyone nodded eagerly. Even Sammy Sailor!

"But will you be able to find Dinah Doll?" Miss Pink Cat asked Noddy anxiously. "And even if you do, how are you going to persuade her to come back?"

"Don't worry, I'll find her!" Noddy said with determination. "And I've got a brilliant idea to make her want to stay in Toyland..."

Noddy hurried off to find Mr Sparks, who really was a good artist.

"Would you please paint a special sign for Dinah Doll's stall as a sort of 'Welcome Back' present?" Noddy asked him breathlessly.

"Of course I will!" Mr Sparks replied. "Toy Town needs Dinah Doll!"

Noddy then sped towards the station, hoping to find
Dinah Doll there.

Dinah was at the station but she was ready to board
the very next train. If Noddy did not arrive soon, he
would miss her!

Luckily, Dinah met Big-Ears at the station and he
delayed her a little. Otherwise, they might never have
seen her again!

"Oh Dinah! I'm so glad I've found you!" Noddy panted when he arrived. "Please come back and open your stall again!"

"I'm afraid no one wants my stall any more, Noddy," Dinah Doll told him sadly. "They just want Sammy Sailor's stall."

"No they don't!" Noddy insisted. "All the toys want your stall. And we've got a special surprise for you, to show how much we all want you back!"

The train was just about to leave and Dinah Doll asked Noddy if he would help her with her suitcase. "You're not catching the train are you, Dinah?" Noddy pleaded.

"No," she smiled broadly. "I'm going back with you and Big-Ears to Market Square!"

Everyone cheered as Noddy drove Dinah Doll back to
Market Square.

"Hooray!" shouted Mr Wobbly Man.

"Hooray!" shouted Jumbo. "I'm fed up with these
stupid paintings," he added. "I just want to buy
something nice from Dinah Doll's stall!"

All the toys gathered round as Dinah Doll opened her stall again.

"It's good to have you back, Dinah!" Mr Tubby Bear shouted.

"Hear! Hear!" all the others joined in.

Mr Sparks and Miss Pink Cat looked on excitedly as Dinah Doll pulled back the cloth.

Underneath was the special surprise Noddy had asked Mr Sparks to paint!

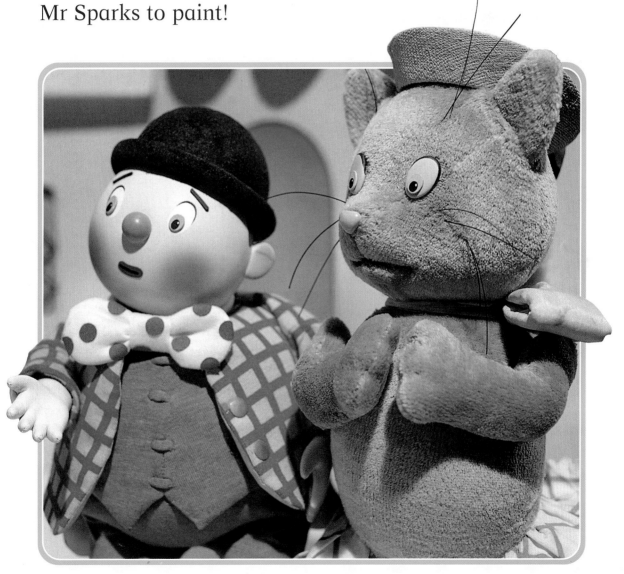

"I wonder what it is?" Dinah Doll said eagerly as she pulled away the cloth.

"Oh, my very own stall sign!" she exclaimed joyfully. "How wonderful! Oh thank you, all my dear friends!"

"May I be the first to buy something from your stall with a new sign?" Noddy chuckled.

"Of course, Noddy!" Dinah Doll replied. "You can have anything you want!"

"But you don't have to buy it, Noddy," Dinah Doll added with a smile.

"You can have it as a present! If it weren't for you, after all, I wouldn't be back here amongst all my friends!"

This edition first published in Great Britain by HarperCollins Publishers Ltd in 2000

1 3 5 7 9 10 8 6 4 2

Copyright © 1999 Enid Blyton Ltd. Enid Blyton's signature mark and the words
"NODDY" and "TOYLAND" are Registered Trade Marks of Enid Blyton Ltd.
For further information on Enid Blyton please contact www.blyton.com

ISBN: 0 00 136183 X

Reproduction by Graphic Studio S.r.l. Verona
Printed in Italy by Garzanti Verga S.r.l.

MORE NODDY BOOKS FOR YOU TO ENJOY

Noddy and the Bouncing Ball

Noddy is Caught in a Storm

Noddy and the Driving Lesson

Noddy is Far Too Busy

Noddy and the Goblins

Noddy and the Magic Watch

Noddy and the Noisy Drum

Noddy the Nurse

Noddy and the Singing Bush

Noddy Tells a Story

Noddy Tidies Toyland

Noddy znd the Treasure Map